SO-BUA-659

The Circus

AN EARLY BIRD BOOK™

Written by Wendy Boase
Illustrated by Deborah Ward

Random House 🏠 New York

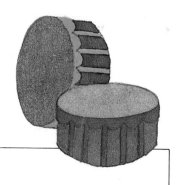

Here are two clowns.
Can you see them?

Here is the human
cannonball.
What is he hiding in?

Here is the strong man.
Can you find him?

Here is the acrobat.
Can you see her?

Here is the man on
the flying trapeze.
Where is he hiding?

Here is the juggler.
What is she hiding in?

The ringmaster calls
all his performers.
"Time for the show,"
he says.

The man on the flying trapeze
swings high in the air.

The acrobat bounces
backward, over and
over again.

The clowns play
funny tricks
on each other.

The strong man shows
everyone how strong he is.

The juggler juggles
five clubs at once.

The human cannonball
flies through the air
while the audience
cheers and claps.